BUMPER CHRISTMAS ISSUE

ALL THE NEWS AND VIEWS FROM THE FROZEN NORTH

Mark Burgess

The views expressed in this magazine are not necessarily those of the Editor or contributors. While every effort has been made to verify facts, no responsibility can be taken for errors that have crept in uninvited.

Scholastic Children's Books,
Scholastic Publications Ltd,
7–9 Pratt Street, London NW1 0AE, UK

Scholastic Inc.,
730 Broadway, New York, NY 10003, USA

Scholastic Canada Ltd,
123 Newkirk Road, Richmond Hill,
Ontario, Canada L4C 3G5

Ashton Scholastic Pty Ltd,
P O Box 579, Gosford, New South Wales,
Australia

Ashton Scholastic Ltd,
Private Bag 1, Penrose, Auckland,
New Zealand

First published by Scholastic Publications Ltd,
1993

ISBN 0 590 55338 0

Typeset by Contour Typesetters, Southall,
London
Printed by Cox & Wyman Ltd, Reading,
Berks.

10 9 8 7 6 5 4 3 2 1

HO HO HO!

CONTENTS

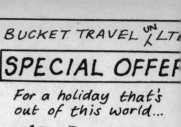

Hi, *Ho, Ho, Ho!* readers! Welcome to this bumper issue of the magazine that's 'black and white and read all the way through', ha ha. And it's packed full of . . . er, things. Sorry, my memory's not what it used to be. The doctor gave me some pills for 'memory loss' but I keep forgetting to take them! Now, where was I? Oh, yes, there was something important I meant to say at this point. I wrote a note to remind me. I wonder where I put it. Oh, bother, now my pen's run out – and it's left the door open. Excuse me, I'll have to shut it – there's a chill wind blowing today. Come to think of it, there's always a chill wind blowing as this is the Frozen North – 'the land where snow reigns', ha, ha. I keep asking the production team if we can move the *Ho, Ho Ho!* offices a bit nearer the Equator, but they just give me icy looks. Oh, well . . . Good gracious! I've remembered – that thing, the important one I meant to say earlier – it's . . . Happy Christmas! That's it! *HAPPY CHRISTMAS!* And have lots of fun reading *Ho, Ho, Ho!* too!

Best wishes,

Anne Kneesia

IN CIRCLES

The Arctic Magic Circle met last Wednesday directly above the centre of the Earth. Wizards and witches descended on the area, which subsequently suffered a severe cold spell. It is not known which witch or wizard it was due to. Later an enormous scarf was found around the North Pole. The Polar Police are still trying to unravel the mystery.

PLUMBING THE HEIGHTS

The huge snowball which landed on Big Ben in London last week has begun to thaw. Some flooding is expected and plumbers are working round the clock to tackle the problem. A spokesperson said it was proving a drain on their resources but they were bearing up well under the pressure.

DOCTOR QUACK

Doctor, Doctor, you must help me!

What is it?

I've swallowed a roll of film!

mmm...

We'll just have to wait and see what develops!!

CHRISTMAS TREE MYSTERY

Special Branch have admitted that they are no closer to solving the mysterious appearance of a 100ft Christmas tree in Tinseltown High Street. Chief Inspector Fussle, who was recovering from being hit on the head by a falling candle but made light of it, promised that his men were doing all they could. Forty of his best officers were digging for clues at that very moment and he expected to get to the root of the problem before nightfall.

TICKETS UP

The price of pantomime tickets is expected to rise dramatically this season after panto actors staged demonstrations. Cinderella said she was seeking redress, Puss-in-Boots walked off and Jack and the Beanstalk received insufficient support. Audiences booed and hissed repeatedly during performances. *The Giant's Nose*, a new play by Willie Pickett, has closed after a shorter run than expected.

7

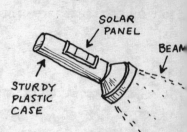

During the Christmas period the weather forecast is:

THE NORTH
It will be dark with quite a bit of snow.

THE SOUTH
It will be light with quite a bit of snow.

IN BETWEEN
It will be sometimes light, sometimes dark, with some snow in some places but sunny periods in others with temperatures varying considerably. Possibly wind, rain and other sorts of weather as well.

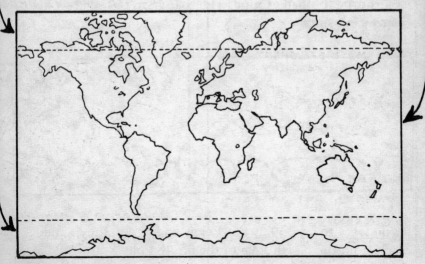

THIS WEATHER FORECAST WAS BROUGHT TO YOU BY: GLOBAL WARNING INC.

CURIOUS FACTS AND FEATS

The largest Christmas pudding ever was made by Ethel Blubber-Smythe of Colnthorpe in 1924. Colnthorpe United, the local football team, manfully ate as much as they could; the remainder was used to resurface the approach to Colnthorpe football ground. The road hasn't needed resurfacing since.

If you were to lay 350,394,881 eggs end to end they would reach from the North Pole to the South Pole. You would also need to be a chicken.

On Christmas Day 1879, Sidney Sprockett of Adelaide
succeeded in balancing 49 parrots, 19 cockatoos and a
kookaburra on his nose for 17 hours 34 minutes.

The most ridiculous Christmas decoration was made by Miss
L. Tow of Manhattan in 1899. It was finally dismantled by the
Police Department in 1945.

EXCLUSIVE:
SANTA
A NIGHT IN THE LIFE

Frank N. Quirey interviews The Man Himself just after his Big Night

FNQ: Let me first say what a privilege it is to be allowed this exclusive interview with you, Santa, in your special secret North Pole hideout and on this, the very day after your Big Night . . . Santa? . . . Santa?

SC: zzzzzzzzz . . . zzzzzzzz . . . Eh?

FNQ: I was saying what a privilege it is to interview you, today of all days.

SC: Oh! *Today of all days!*

FNQ: Yes, and it's really kind of you to agree to it.

SC: You mean I agreed to it?

FNQ: Yes, last week.

SC: Oh, *last* week. That explains it.

FNQ: So, then, Santa – I know all our readers will be longing

to know this: how do you do it? . . . Santa? . . . Santa?

SC: zzzzzzz . . . zzzz . . . Eh? Do what?

FNQ: How do you deliver presents to children all over the world in one night?

SC: Do I do that? Oh, yes, I remember . . . Well, it takes organisation. You wouldn't believe the organisation it takes.

FNQ: Will you tell us about the organisation?

SC: Nope.

FNQ: Why not?

SC: As I said, you wouldn't believe it.

FNQ: I must say, it must be pretty amazing to do all that in one single night.

SC: Yes, I suppose you could say that.

FNQ: And all those chimneys!

SC: Ah, well, there you are. Chimneys aren't what they used to be. In fact, there aren't many chimneys about these days – not what you'd call sootable – ho, ho! But I never really needed chimneys in the first place. Magic's the thing, or to give it its technical name, I.N.S.T.A.N.T., which stands for Inter-Stocking-Time-Arrested-Nocturnal-Transfer.

Einstein put me onto it, and very useful it is, too – there are a lot more people in the world these days.

FNQ: So what exactly is I.N.S.T.A.N.T.?

SC: Well, put simply, it's 'here today – there today', all in a split second. I'll show you, if you like.

FNQ: Yes, please!

SC: There, done it.

FNQ: But you haven't moved.

SC: Well, I didn't *appear* to. It's so quick. Roughly 48 billion miles a second.

FNQ: All right, then, so where did you go?

SC: Oh, just outside. I put a Christmas pudding in the glove compartment of your car. I'm sorry, I squashed it a bit. So there's proof for you – go and look.

(*Later*)

FNQ: It's true! Amazing! Tell me, Santa, this I.N.S.T.A.N.T. thing, is it tiring? Do you need a rest afterwards? . . . Santa? . . . Santa?

SC: zzzzzzzz . . . zzzzzzzzz . . .

15

Inside Camp Christmas

Santa's North Pole Hideout
photographed by Luke Sharpe

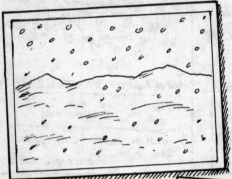

From the outside you'd never know it was there!

A sliding door reveals the main entrance. The security officer checks in all visitors →

All the accommodation is very comfortable.

This is the main control room. Letters are sorted and present quotas allocated.

Gifts are carefully wrapped by hand before being sent to the distribution warehouse.

Sacks ready for loading beside the launch ramp — this is where Santa's Big Night really starts!

ADVERTISEMENT

Santa used to be completely elf-reliant but now he's looking
for more helpers. Would *you* measure up (4ft 2in MAX)?
Successful applicants will receive full training at Santa's
Secret North Pole hideout with diplohohohomas being
awarded on completion of the course.
Interested? Then don't delay, apply today!
All applications must be posted up the chimney by December
2nd.

ESSENTIAL EQUIPMENT

Mobile Computer-phone

The latest technology allows each
helper to keep in touch with the Control room.
The presents are collected from the
warehouse and, after wrapping and
labelling, are sorted according to
destination ready for the Big Night.

Scissors

The presents are
wrapped in the
traditional way.

Ribbon

Labels

Special disappearing labels are
used to identify the presents.
They vanish once the parcels
have been delivered.

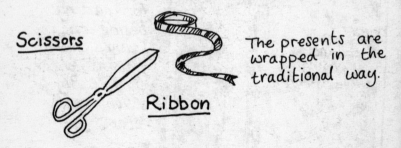

UNIFORM

This special uniform is provided on completion of the course.

Hat
with reinforced top to guard against falling presents.
Colours: red.

Badge
For identification purposes - Security is tight at the North Pole.

Jacket
in a choice of green or green.

Belt
for belting up when absolute quiet is required.

Breeches
Fundamental clothing.

Shoes
From an ancient but surprisingly practical design

Bells
Totally useless - just for decoration

Normal working hours until December when overtime is required. Annual holiday: June. Perks: Free air travel and unlimited Christmas gift allowance.

CHRISTMAS QUIZ

If you're feeling a little down in the mouth after Christmas dinner (you probably forgot to pluck the turkey), liven things up again with this quiz.

1. What is the biggest hat in the world?
2. What carol did the three wise men sing?
3. Why are there only twenty-five letters in the alphabet at Christmas?
4. What nationality is Santa Claus?
5. When is a Christmas pudding musical?
6. Why can't you starve at the seaside?
7. What are ducks called at Christmas?
8. What do you call a crazy cat that's just eaten a Christmas quacker?
9. What game do frogs play at Christmas?
10. What currency is used at the North Pole?
11. Why should you wear a tartan waistcoat at Christmas?
12. What dinosaur lived at the North Pole?
13. What does Santa do in his garden?
14. Where do sheep have their hair cut?
15. Why do bald men spend Christmas out of doors?

16. What invention enables you to see through the thickest walls?
17. What game do cows like to play at Christmas parties?
18. What has two humps and is found at the North Pole?
19. What do monkeys sing at Christmas time?
20. Where do snowmen and women dance?

ANSWERS

1. The polar ice cap.
2. 'Oh, camel ye faithful.'
3. Because the angel said, 'No-L'.
4. North Polish.
5. When it's piping hot.
6. Because of the sand which is there.
7. Christmas quackers.
8. A duck-filled batty-puss.
9. Croquet.
10. Iced lolly.
11. To keep your tummy in check.
12. The diplohohodocus.
13. Hoe, hoe, hoe.
14. At the baa-baa's.
15. To get some fresh hair.
16. The window.
17. Moosical chairs.
18. A lost camel.
19. 'Jungle bells'.
20. At a snowball.

★ START ➡

CHRISTMAS MORNING AND YOU FORGOT TO WRAP YOUR PRESENTS!

BACK ONE PLACE

➡

SOMEONE SUGGESTS YOU ALL PLAY A GAME.

EVERYBODY BACK TO START!

⬆

A FAMILY GAME...

MONOTONY

IT'S RELATIVELY GOOD FUN & GOES ON & ON & ON!

UNCLE JOE FINISHES HIS JOKE!

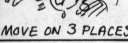

MOVE ON 3 PLACES

⬆

YOU ASK AUNT MABEL HOW SHE IS. SHE TELLS YOU.

MISS 3 TURNS

⬅

GRANDMA ARRIVES AND GIVES YOU JUST WHAT YOU DESERVE.

ANOTHER TURN

UNCLE JOE BEGINS TO TELL A JOKE...

GO BACK 3 PLACES

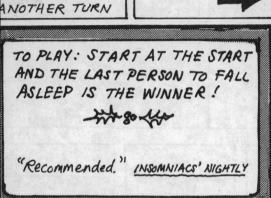

TO PLAY: START AT THE START AND THE LAST PERSON TO FALL ASLEEP IS THE WINNER!

"Recommended." INSOMNIACS' NIGHTLY

CHRISTMAS LUNCH IS BURNT TO A CINDER.

BACK ONE PLACE

GRANDPA MAKES A RUDE NOISE.

EVERYBODY MISS A TURN

THE DOG IS SICK

THROW AGAIN

Harriet Husky at the Pole

A PARTLY TRUE STORY IN SEVERAL PARTS

PART 439

AND ARRIVED NOT A MOMENT TOO SOON...

HI, MY NAME'S ANDREW HELP. CALL ME 'ANDY.' ANYTHING I CAN DO?

YES, ACTUALLY...

YOU'RE LUCKY I WASN'T FAR AWAY.

AS THEY SPED OFF ON THE SNOWMOBILE, HARRIET TOLD ANDY HER STORY...

TO BEGIN WITH I LOST IT IN RIO...

...SO THEN OF COURSE I WENT TO THE LOST PROPERTY OFFICE AND THEY TOLD ME TO ASK...

PEN PALS

Dear *Ho Ho Ho!*

I've just received my issue of *Ho Ho Ho!* from three years ago, dropped in by a tramper on the Heaphy Track. I really like your article on keeping in touch with relatives worldwide and what I'd like to know is, are there any distant cousins of mine out there? If so, me and mum would like to hear from you. Please write!

> Bette 'You thought we were extinct' Moa,
> That scrubby bit of bush on the left,
> Lower Heaphy,
> New Zealand.

P.S. Also, the article 'I am John's Umbrella' looked really interesting, but the page has been torn out of my mag. Can you send me a copy?

It's on it's way, Bette, together with a Ho Ho Ho! T-shirt for you and your mum!

A REAL KNOCKOUT

Dear Mister Letturs,

I dunt usually rite to maggurzines (I dunt usually rite) but when I furst saw yer maggurzine it nocked me fur six. My bruther wus hitti me wiv it at the time. I had to tell yoo it is really stunnin. Plez send me sum more cos I promissed to get him for it. Oh yeh, here is a joak fur yoo. Knock, nock. Yoo say hoos thur. I say Arfur. Arfur hoo, yoo say. Arfur minnit, I carnt remember the rest.

Yurs trolly
Spud Ogre

Our 'Bumper' issue is on its way, Spud!

A PRICKLY CUSTOMER?

Dear *Ho Ho Ho!*

I'm not one to complain but I felt I just had to protest at the unfair treatment of hedgehogs in your recent issues. Me and my flatmate are in total agreement that your jokes have gone too far. Jokes about hairbrushes are all very well but chickens cross roads too, you know. We hedgehogs are loving, cuddly creatures, not the objects of ridicule you portray.

Name and address supplied

We're all sorry here at Ho Ho Ho! We didn't mean to be so unfeeling: your letter certainly pricked our consciences – oops! Sorry, there we go again! No more hedgehog jokes, we promise. Please accept a Ho Ho Ho! 'Neverburst' hot water bottle with our compliments.

BOWLED OVER

Dear *Ho Ho Ho!*

Thank you so much for the article on snowmen and women in a recent issue of your magazine. It really showed us snowpeople in our true colours and not, as so often portrayed, as pale, insignificant creatures that simply melt into the background. Your warm and friendly article will have thawed many a heart.

Wendy Springcums

THE FIRST CHRISTMAS TREE

Rudolph tells the full illuminating story

'Ruldoph', said the Editor last Tuesday, 'I want a story about Christmas trees – you write it!' So I was lumbered with the job. Just like that. What do I know about Christmas trees? Hardly anything. Though actually, now I think of it, my family has had a long association with the things. I'll tell you about it.

It all began a long time ago in Germany. A distant ancestor of mine called Rudolfus (he had a nose just as red as mine) lived there with his family in a big wood. Well, one day a woodcutter was walking through the wood. It was just before Christmas and he was looking for holly and ivy and suchlike with which to

decorate his home. When he came to the part of the wood where my ancestor Rudolfus lived, he suddenly saw a little fir tree with what appeared to be a glowing light on it – though really it was Rudolfus hiding behind the tree, and the light was his red nose. 'What a lovely Christmas decoration!' thought the woodcutter. 'I'll take it home.' Well, of course Rudolfus ran off the moment the woodcutter approached. The man was very disappointed, but he took the tree home anyway and later had the idea of putting candles on it to remind him of how he'd first seen it.

Well, it wasn't long before everybody in the woodcutter's village wanted a Christmas tree, and then the next village and so on until they had spread all over the world. Needless to say, it was a growth industry and all sorts of people branched out into the Christmas tree business, selling baubles and tinsel as well as candles, and that's how the trees were decorated for hundreds of years.

Then in 1882 an employee of the General Electric Company had a bright idea. The light bulb had just been invented and this chap thought, why not put them on Christmas trees? So he goes and tells the General about his idea and General Electric beams at him and says, 'Well done, Watt,' (or whatever his name was), and that's how we got lights on Christmas trees, all because of my ancestor Rudolfus.

Mary Fairy ✿❅✿

Poetry Postbag

Thanks to all those readers who sent in their poems. Here are the best from this month's sackful.

SNOWFLAKES BY I.C. WETHER

I like to watch the snowflakes fall
  All downwards, in a flutter,
Like daisies going to a ball,
  Or sliced white bread and butter.
The loveliest sight I ever saw,
  So quiet, all a-hush –
And then the rain begins to pour
  And everywhere there's slush.

POME BY SPUD OGRE

I fort Ide rite a littul pome
   On my speshul gardun nome.
I tride to rite upon his shirt,
   He didn't like it coz it hurt.
So then I rote upon sum snow.
   My pen it stopt, it woodnt go.
The thing wos froz, at least I fink
   That that woz it, becos iced ink.

PETE THE EXPLORER BY EGON CRAZIE

A polar explorer named Pete
Had nothing at all left to eat,
So he ate *Ho, Ho, Ho!*
– It's nutitious, you know –
(When served with fried rice and a sweet).

Alas, it was all Pete could do
To get only just halfway through,
For the jokes, I've no doubt,
Kept him falling about
And he bit off too much to chew!

CHRISTMAS BY I.M.A. MISERIE

Christmas comes but once a year,
   Jolly good, I say.
Carol singers knock the door –
   I wish they'd go away.
That awful chap in red and white,
   My word, it's really shocking –
He creeps about on Christmas night
   Stuffing every stocking!
And then there's all the ghastly food –
   The Christmas cake and pud.
Get rid of Christmas Day, I say –
   DO AWAY WITH IT FOR GOOD!

Oops, this one got in by mistake. Sorry! Ed.

CHRISTMAS COOKING

BROWNIES

Brownies are what trolls eat at Christmas. Goblins like gobbling them as well, if there are any left after the trolls have been at them, that is. This is enough for one troll or eight goblins:

fat for greasing
125g self-raising flour
a pinch of salt
100g butter
100g plain chocolate
100g granulated sugar
1 egg
1 teaspoon vanilla essence
100g chopped walnuts or pecans

Grease a 20cm square baking tin and line the bottom with greaseproof paper. In a medium-sized saucepan melt the butter and the chocolate (heat it gently), then remove from the heat and add the sugar. Beat the egg and then stir into the chocolate mixture. Sift together the flour and the salt and then add to the chocolate mixture, along with the vanilla essence and chopped nuts. Mix well and wish (that there aren't any trolls watching!). Then spread the mixture evenly in the tin. Bake in the oven at 180°C, Gas 4, for 35–40 minutes. Leave the tin to cool before cutting into squares. Don't overcook brownies – they should be moist and soft inside: that's the way trolls like them. Delicious!

with Pattie Kake

PUNCH

Punch is what boxers drink at Christmas, especially on
Boxing Day, though you don't have to be a boxer to drink it.
You can be a poodle, or a husky, or anything, really. It's a
great drink: serve it at your Christmas party, either hot or
cold.

1 tin pineapple chunks
1 pawful of glacé cherries
500ml water
200g sugar
1 litre pineapple or orange juice (or a mixture of the two)
1 teaspoon ground ginger
1 teaspoon ground cinnamon
10 cloves

Open the tin of pineapple and drain off the juice into a
saucepan. Add the sugar, water and spices. Bring gently to
the boil, stirring constantly, then boil for 5 minutes. Add the
fruit juice. Cut the pineapple and glacé cherries into quarters
and add to the liquid. Reheat gently to serve hot; or cool and
then chill in the fridge to serve cold.

THE HO HO HO! CHRISTMAS PLATE

A COLLECTOR'S ITEM
SPECIALLY CREATED
BY CLAY MOLDER
FOR THIS
CHRISTMAS

TWICE ACTUAL SIZE

A PLATE TO
TREASURE
FOR ALWAYS
(UNLESS YOU DROP IT)

LIMITED EDITION
OF 1,250,746 APPROX.

PRE-GLAZING OFFER 10% OFF

SEND YOUR ORDER TO Ho, Ho, Ho! BOX 258, NORTH POLE

☆ LITTLE JOEY ☆

MA, IS IT REALLY CHRISTMAS EVE — WHEN SANTA COMES?

YES, DEAR.

YIPEE!

NIGHT, NIGHT, MA!

43

A Christmas ghost story by Jilly Spine

It was Christmas Eve. It was dark. It was cold. Very cold. So cold, even the ice was freezing. The carol singers had given up and gone home on their bicycles. They were all two-tyred. There were no customers at Ivor's Diner so it had closed early. The wind whistled in the chimney.

'Stop that whistling!' shouted Ivor Tummiake as he threw another log on the fire. 'Always the same tune. Don't you know anything else?'

Suddenly there was a ghostly knock at the door.

'Who's that?' said Ivor.

'A ghost, I expect,' said Nora Carrot, the cook. 'Open the door and see.'

Ivor opened the door. Sure enough, there was a ghost.

'Helloooooo,' said the ghost. 'I'd like something to drink. A brandy, I think.'

'We're closed,' said Ivor. 'And anyway, we don't serve spirits.'

'Well, perhaps something to eat, then?' pleaded the ghost.

'Oh, all right, as it's Christmas,' said Ivor; and the ghost came in and sat down at a table.

'Have you got any turkey?' asked the ghost. 'I saw a man eating turkey here yesterday.'

'That's nothing,' said Ivor. 'They had a man-eating Christmas pudding at Bill's Café last week. Caused quite a stir, I can tell you. Nora, how's the turkey?'

Nora stuck her head round the kitchen door. 'The turkey's off.'

'What do you mean, it's off? I only got it on Friday.'

'Well, it's just made a bolt for the door.'

'Clever turkey, that; did metalwork at school.'

At that moment the turkey ran into the room and started swearing.

'Get back in the kitchen this instant!' yelled Ivor. 'Sorry, sir,' he said to the ghost. 'You'll have to excuse the fowl language.'

The turkey ran out of the door and off down the street.

'There,' said Nora. 'Now it's gone off completely. How about a little ghoulash for the gentleman, or there's spookhetti followed by ice cream, I scream and I scream again.'

'Sounds lovely,' said the ghost. 'And will you put on some music? A haunting melody, perhaps?'

'Certainly sir,' said Ivor and went to turn on the radio.

The moment that Ivor's back was turned, the ghost leapt up and tried to grab the money from the till. But he made a grave mistake. Nora was ready for him. She dashed out of the kitchen and, whacking him over the head, laid him out cold.

'I always keep a spirit level handy,' she said. 'You never know when it might be useful.'

Ivor telephoned the Police Station. Fortunately there was a skeleton staff on duty and they sent round an Inn-Spectre Inspector straight away. The ghost was arrested.

'How did you know he was going to rob us?' Ivor asked Nora afterwards.

'Ghosts!' said Nora. 'Ha! I see through them every time.'

Sleigh Sky Test

Bob Uppendown test flies the best sleighs available around the world:

THE GLÜCK & SPLUTTER 'CLASSIC' MK II

STILL IN PRODUCTION AFTER 200 YEARS THIS OLD-STYLE SLEIGH PERFORMS WELL, IS STURDILY BUILT & RELIABLE, THOUGH SURELY IT'S TIME TO RING THE CHANGES WITH THE DECORATION? ✱✱✱✱

THE HOLDFAST 'COMPANION'

RATHER UNEXCITING BUT NEVER-THE-LESS A GOOD ALL-ROUND PERFORMER. THE CHICKEN-POWER OPTION FOR CHEEP RUNNING MAKES IT IDEAL FOR THE FIRST TIME BUYER: ✱✱✱

THE MOLLUSK MAJOR 'BOMBAST'

THIS CURIOUSITY IS REALLY ONLY FOR THE DETERMINED COLLECTOR.
A COMPLETE FAILURE AT LOOP-THE-LOOP AND RATHER SLUGGISH
OTHERWISE, IT HAS NO WEATHER PROTECTION WHATSOEVER ✳✳

THE DRONGO 'STARFLASH' GTX

WONDERFUL - A SLEIGH FOR THE 21ST CENTURY. ZERO DRAG
AND TURBO-CHARGING GIVES SPEED WITH THE MINIMUM OF
EFFORT. A MUST FOR THE SERIOUS HIGH FLIER. ✳✳✳✳✳

DID YOU KNOW . . .

Little-known facts about Christmas Past

The origins of Christmas go back a long way before 1 BC.
The Romans celebrated 'Saturnalia' at the end of the year,
often confused with another Roman festival, 'Paraffinalia',
which was when they'd run out of oil, and whence comes the
well-known Christmas saying, 'No-oil, No-oil'. In Northern
Europe, this mid-winter festival was called Yule and coincided
with the start of the football season; hence expressions like
'Season's Beatings', 'Snow-Goal' and that familiar football
carol, 'Yule Never Walk Alone.'

Before the advent of the Christmas tree, people in North America used to decorate moose antlers with fairy lights or candles. As you might expect, this made the moose pretty furious and led to the expression, 'Hoppy Cross Moose'. People soon got fed up with decorating the moose as he wouldn't stay still and ruined the TV reception.

Christmas puddings were originally boiled in the washing tub. Odds and ends of clothing would get mixed in, and the loose change, buttons, etc. incorporated in the pudding gave rise to the popular custom of including trinkets for luck. This still continues today, although few people include items of clothing.

Deer Donner

The reindeer with a world of experience answers your letters.

Deer Donner,
Mum says I should work hard to pass my eggsams but I'd rather go dancing chick to chick. It's boring laying around at home the whole time. Going out is much more eggciting. What do you think?

Miss Henny Penny

Frankly, Henny Penny, your mother's right. Growing up is no yoke and you'll miss out on all sorts of things if you fluff your eggsams. Your mother has shelled out a lot for your eggucation so get on with your henwork. You don't want a last minute scramble.

Deer Donner,
You will have to excuse my slow writing. I started this lettuce, I mean letter, just after Christmas and it's Easter already. Now the summer holidays are over I'm looking forward to Christmas, though I'm still unwrapping my presents from last year. Happy New Summer Holiday!

Terry Tortoise

Thanks for your letter, Terry. What was your question? (No hurry, now.)

Deer Donner,
Somehow I seem to have written to the wrong magazine. In fact I'm really rather lost altogether as I don't think I'm where I should be and I don't know where that is anyway. Can you help?

Yours anxiously,
Humphrey

You'd be surprised how common your problem is, Humphrey. Only last week I had to put a railway train back on the right track. My advice is to take the Trans-Polar Express to the North Pole. From there you can't go wrong. Just go South.

Deer Donner,
I'm trying to organise a party for some snowfriends of mine. As they live in a field there may be some cows at the party as well. Have you got any suggestions, as I haven't organised a party before?

Shirley Wintersear

The best thing is to have a Snowball. Play 'Take your Pick' – that'll break the ice; then 'Moosical Chairs' – cows love playing that. You could have ice burgers to eat, and invite Santa along – then you can all sing 'Freeze a jolly good fellow'!

Deer Donner,
We're going away for Christmas. My Dad says it's the best
thing for us as it will be getting a bit hot for us around here.
Seems funny to me as it's winter. The only trouble is, we're
not sure where to go. My Dad says, Have you any ideas?

A. Turkey

*You might try Easter Island: I should think that would be a pretty safe bet.
Avoid Greece at all costs.*

Deer Donner,
I'm not a reindeer, or any sort of deer (although my mummy
calls me a little one) but I'd like to learn to fly. Can you tell me
what to do?

Horace Potamus

*I know there was going to be a Hippo Flying School near where you live,
Horace, but I don't think it got off the ground. If you're determined to give
flying a go, drop in at Santa's Flying School and we'll see what we can do.*

PollyPenguin

CROSSWORD

Across

1 A white Christmas?
4 A fruit
7 Christmas trees have them – for sewing?
8 Work with a spade
9 Curved structure
11 Ask to a party
13 Part of a tree
14 Old
17 Request, beg
18 Christmas lights
20 'One– . . . open sleigh'
21 Parts of a book

Down

1 Christmas visitor
2 A single thing
3 Old name for Christmas
4 Not present!
5 Flaming food for Christmas
6 Bird of prey
10 Pull it and – bang!
12 Frozen spike
13 Sand by the sea
15 Cleans with a cloth
16 Game crocodiles play?
19 Put one in a stocking!

CHRISTMAS ☆ FUN

SILENT NIGHT!

TRY THIS TRICK ON A FRIEND — PINCH HIS OR HER NOSE TOGETHER GENTLY AND THEY WON'T BE ABLE TO HUM A THING!

Through the Christmas Card

THROUGH THE CHRISTMAS CARD

Have you ever wanted to walk through a Christmas card?
Well, amaze your friends – here's how you can do it!

Any Christmas card will do, but make sure it's an old one that
nobody wants.

With the card folded, cut
along the lines shown in the
drawing (1). The closer you
cut the easier the trick will be.
Be careful not to cut too far.

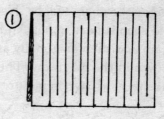

Now cut along the fold (2),
between the two end cuts. You
can now gently open out the
card – and walk through the
hole!

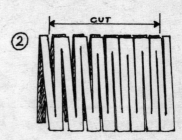

A CHRISTMAS PAPER CHAIN

All you need to make this paper chain is some thin coloured paper, glue and scissors. First cut squares of paper about 10cm square. The more squares you have the longer the chain will be. Next fold each square in half, in half again and then diagonally as shown in the diagrams. Then cut slits as shown in picture (4).

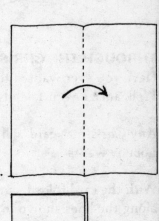

1.

2.

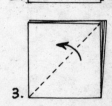

3.

Now carefully open out the squares and lay them flat. Take the first square and put a little glue in each of the four corners (5). Lay the next square on top and press down the corners, then put some glue in the centre (6). Lay a third square on top and press it down. This square then has glue in the corners, the next in the middle and so on until all the squares are stuck together.

You can now open out the chain by gently pulling it apart. A small piece of sticky tape on each end will help you do this.

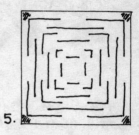

5.

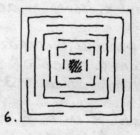

6.

RUDOLF

THE BOSS SAID I COULD HAVE THE WEEK OFF BEFORE THE BIG NIGHT

TIME GOES SO QUICKLY WHEN YOU'RE ENJOYING YOURSELF — IT'S ALREADY...

DECEMBER 24TH!

PARTY HATS

All you need to make these party hats is some thin card, sticky tape, a ruler and scissors — and your paintbox.

Each hat is made from a piece of card about 25 cm x 35 cm

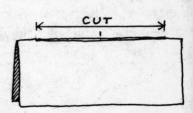

Fold it in half lengthways:

Draw a line along the fold and find the centre. Mark off 14 cm each side of this and then cut along the line so that you end up with a slit 28 cm long.

Now you can design your hat. With the fold at the bottom, draw an outline of the shape you want:

Like this for a pirate hat:

Or this for a crown :-

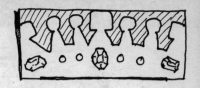

Then cut it out but be careful not to cut off any of the fold.

Now you can paint the hat. When it is quite dry, stick a small piece of tape across each end of the slit, inside and out - this should stop the hat tearing when you put it on.

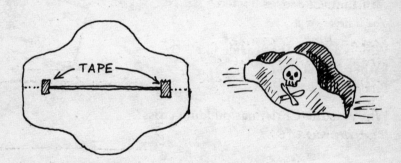

TAPE

Other designs you might try:

Santa's hat

Bowler hat

Jester's hat

Why couldn't the sailors play cards at Christmas?
Because the captain was standing on the deck.

Have you heard the joke about the Christmas
card that was never posted?
You'll never get it.

Why is a cat at the seaside like
Father Christmas?
Because of its sandy claws.

Why was the Christmas pudding cross?
It was steaming.

What do you call a monster with mince pies stuck in its ears?
Anything you like, it can't hear you.

GRANDMA: I've been making mince pies since before you were born.
DAN: This must be one of them.

Is it true that owls don't care about Christmas?
Yes, they don't give a hoot.

What cake shouldn't you eat at Christmas?
A cake of soap.

Have you heard the joke about the four-ton mince pie?
It takes some swallowing.

What do you do if a rhino charges you at a Christmas party?
Pay him.

How do you wish a monster 'Happy Christmas'?
From as far away as possible.

Did you hear the joke about the enormous Christmas parcel?
There's nothing in it.

What do you give a man who has everything?
Penicillin.

What did the Christmas card say to the stamp?
Stick with me and we'll go places.

How do you make a Mexican chilli?
Take him to the North Pole.

Why was Cinderella dropped from the football team?
She kept running away from the ball.

What is a ghost's favourite Christmas entertainment?
A phantomime.

What's the best thing to put in a mince pie?
Your teeth.

Why shouldn't you invite a herd of cows to your Christmas party?
There'd be udder chaos.

Where do you get a Christmas present for your dog?
British Bone Stores.

What did the witch want for Christmas?
A spell at the seaside.

How do hedgehogs kiss
under the mistletoe?
Carefully!

I PROTEST!
NO MORE
HEDGEHOG JOKES!

In which tree might you find a Christmas cake?
A pantry.

Where should you look for a Christmas present for a cat?
In a catalogue.

How do you make your Christmas money go a long way?
Post it to New York.

Who gets the sack at Christmas?
Santa Claus!

69

CHRISTMAS PRESENTS

Do you have trouble finding just the right present? The *Ho Ho Ho!* team have put together this selection from what's on offer around the world this season:

Christmas Eggs

From Easter Island, these hard-boiled decorated eggs are an unbeatable present for the cook of the family.

Storm in a teacup

Invented in Great Britain, a real storm in miniature brews inside the teacup. Conversation piece anywhere.

Musical Rock

Extracted in it's crude form in Canada, this rock emits restful melodies when exposed to the right atmosphere. Entertaining & unusual.

100 year diary

Printed and bound in Greece, this weighty volume is ideal for those that like to plan well ahead. For all ages.

Mystery Gift

Made in Australia, you can give this gift again & again — just the thing if you find choosing presents a problem!

The Brazil-Nut Case

NINE LIVES
DETECTIVE AGENCY

IN THE OFFICE OF THE NINE LIVES DETECTIVE AGENCY, KIT KLEWS, THE FAMOUS DETECTIVE, AND HIS PARTNER, GUY 'THE BIRD', DISCUSS THEIR LATEST AND MOST BAFFLING CASE...

THIS BRAZIL-NUT CASE IS GETTING ME DOWN. IT'S A REAL PUZZLE.

SURE IS BOSS. IT'S A HARD ONE TO CRACK AND NO MISTAKE.

IF ONLY WE HAD SOMETHING TO GO ON...

LIKE A BICYCLE, YOU MEAN, BOSS?

SUDDENLY THE TELEPHONE RANG.

BRING!

IF YOU WANT TO LEARN SOMETHING GO TO 'THE STUMPS', DEAD END LANE.

MYSTERIOUS VOICE

WHO WAS THE MYSTERIOUS CALLER? WHAT WAS THERE AT "THE STUMPS"? THE INTREPID DUO LOST NO TIME—

SWIFTLY THEY SPED THROUGH THE DARK & SILENT STREETS:

AND ARRIVED AT 'THE STUMPS'. IT LOOKED DESERTED.

THEY CREPT UP THE STEPS...

INSIDE A TERRIBLE SIGHT MET THEIR EYES...

THE SIGHT WAS SO TERRIBLE THE ARTIST COULD NOT BEGIN TO DRAW IT. SORRY.

✰✰✰ ✦✦✦ PUZZLES ✦✦✦ ✰✰✰

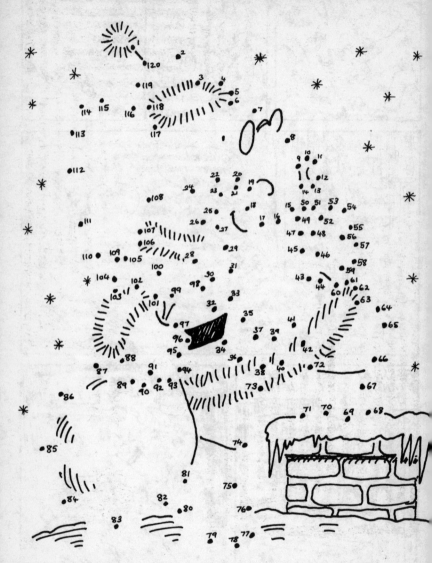

Who is this? Join the dots to find out!

Can you find the right route through the maze to Little Joey's presents?

SPOT THE DIFFERENCE!

CAN YOU FIND THE TEN DIFFERENCES?

PAINTING BY NUMBERS

GET OUT YOUR PAINTS AND COLOUR THE PICTURE!

1 RED	2 GREEN	3 BLUE	4 PINK
5 YELLOW	6 ORANGE	7 VIOLET	8 WHITE

SPOTLIGHT

The spotlight is on Santa, but which is his shadow?

STRETCH
THE PAPER

This is a very simple trick but it looks very clever.

Fold a piece of paper in half. Draw on the shape exactly as shown and cut it out.

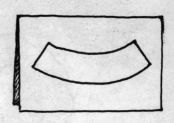

You will now have two paper shapes exactly alike.

Now show everyone the two shapes, one above the other like this:

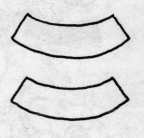

Ask them which is the bigger piece. It's the top one isn't it?

Then you take the bottom piece and pretend to stretch it. Put it back <u>above</u> the other piece and it will now look the larger one. Everyone will be amazed!

MYSTERY CAROL

Follow the footprints through the snow. The first letter of each object will spell out a well-known Christmas carol. What is it?

FUNNY FAMILY

Add the missing bits to this family!

Give everybody a name.

Oops! Somehow the reins have got muddled.

Which belongs to the reindeer?

What's black and white and red all over?
A sun-burnt penguin, of course!
Can you spot him?

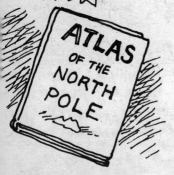

BRICK
OF THE
MONTH
CLUB

LONDON STOCK

LOVELY MIXED COLOURS

PEBBLES AND AIR HOLES

THIS MONTH'S CHOICE

COLLECT BRICKS
A FASCINATING HOBBY

A DIFFERENT BRICK EACH MONTH
ALL CERTIFIED GENUINE

BOTMC, PO BOX 93, CLODTON

GIRAFFE
SCARFS

* HIGH QUALITY *

* VARIOUS COLOURS *

* LONG LASTING *

STRIPES OR SPOTS

* ALSO: KITTENS' MITTENS

NATTY KNITTERS LTD., SKEIN.

SNOW
IN A BOTTLE

REAL ARCTIC SNOW
SPECIALLY SELECTED
AND FREEZE-DRIED

THE BEAUTY OF IT
FOR ALWAYS

THE PERFECT CHRISTMAS GIFT

Joli's BEST
BEARD
WHITENER

GETS RID OF DIRT, SOOT & MINCE PIE STAI

"I never use anything else." S.C

"I never use anything." Spud Og

ANSWERS

p.57

S	N	O	W	Y		A	P	P	L	E
A		N		U		B		U		A
N	E	E	D	L	E	S		D	I	G
T		E		E		D				L
A	R	C	H		I	N	V	I	T	E
		R		I		T		N		
B	R	A	N	C	H		A	G	E	D
E		C		I		S				U
A	S	K		C	A	N	D	L	E	S
C		E		L		A		E		T
H	O	R	S	E		P	A	G	E	S

p.78

p.80 (B) IS SANTA'S SHADOW.

p.76 ELEPHANTA CLAUS!

p.82-83 "GOOD KING WENCESLAS"

p.86 (C) REIN.

p.77

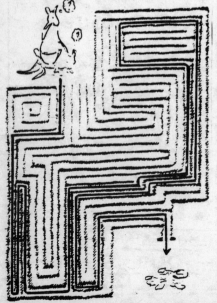